HUNTLEY PUBLIC LIBRARY
P9-DNF-893

ANDREA DAVIS PINKNEY

Fishing Day

Illustrated by
SHANE W. EVANS

Jump at the Sun / Hyperion Books for Children / New York

Especially for Donna and Anne—A.D.P.

For information address Hyperion Books for Children,
114 Fifth Avenue, New York, New York 10011-5690.
First Edition
1 3 5 7 9 10 8 6 4 2
Printed in Singapore
Library of Congress Cataloging-in-Publication Data on file.
ISBN 0-7868-0766-0 (trade ed.)
ISBN 0-7868-2614-2 (lib. ed.)
Visit www.jumpatthesun.com

*Thank you, God. Dedicated to my uncle Booster—thank you for sharing—*S.W.E.

When Saturday comes, Mama and I wake long before the sun, so we can catch the fish right when *they* wake.

"Mama, you up?" I call. But before Mama even answers, I smell hominy cooking in the kitchen.

Mama leans in the doorway of my bedroom. "I *been* up," she says. "Making sure we got us a hot breakfast."

I pull on my overalls and buckle them fast, before the cold has a chance to reach my bones.

In the kitchen, Mama says, "Eat good now, Reenie. We've got a long fishing day ahead."

Mama and me, we sure love fishing. We've got a special fishing place along the north bank of a wide muddy stream folks around here call Jim Crow River.

Mama baits each of our hooks with a kernel of corn from her sack, then casts the rest into the water. We watch the corn pellets float just below the water's surface. We wait for the carp to come along and nibble the tiny jewels of food.

Today the carp aren't taking up our bait.

"Not even a nibble," I say.

"Patience, Reenie," Mama says softly. "Fish can be finicky at the start."

Suddenly a little stone skips across the water. Leaves crunch up behind us. It's Mr. Billy Troop and his boy, Pigeon. Pigeon's not his real true name. His real name is Peter. I call him Pigeon because when he and his daddy come to fish, Pigeon's doing everything but sitting still. He's always flitting somewhere. Just like an up-jumpy bird.

Mr. Troop's got his bucket of bait and two fishing rods. Pigeon races off toward the river's edge, skipping another stone, messing up the water's calm.

Mama shakes her head. "That boy's suffering from want," she says. "It's a shame, too, 'cause all of us—even the fish—suffer from the flurry he makes."

"A shame," I say.

Mama's told mc that Pigeon and his daddy have it harder than most folks. She says they don't fish just for the love of it. They *need* to fish so they can eat.

In all the time we've been fishing alongside Pigeon and his daddy, we've never said a word to them, and they've never said a word to us. Not a word.

Today's no different. At first, the Troops pretend they don't see us. But when I look in Pigeon's direction, he holds on with his eyes, like he wishes he could speak to me. "Watch the water, Reenie," Mama says, her face getting tight.

Mr. Troop puts a hand on Pigeon's back. "Keep with this side of things," he says, all firm.

That's when Mama tells me how the river got its nickname. "Jim Crow is the law of the land," she explains. "The law that says black people have a place, white people have a place, and the two should steer clear of each other."

"But, Mama," I say, "rivers are for everybody."

Mama tries to help me understand. "That's true in nature's eyes, Reenie. But folks who fish have their own ideas. We and white folks have kept our distance here, for as long as memory serves."

Mr. Troop and Pigeon set down their gear on the riverbank, not far from Mama and me. Their voices pierce the dawn.

"Come away from the water, son," Mr. Troop calls. "You'll spook the fish with all that commotion."

"With all that flitting," I say quietly, so only Mama can hear.

Mr. Troop baits his hooks with night crawlers. He and Pigeon never catch any fish with those crawlers. Someone needs to tell them that the crawlers are too scrawny this time of year. That carp like corn and bread balls best.

There's a chilly bite to the air. Mr. Troop has got his cap pulled down low over his eyes. Pigeon's singing "Boggle Mo," a ditty that I'd bet a whole dollar makes the carp want to plug their ears.

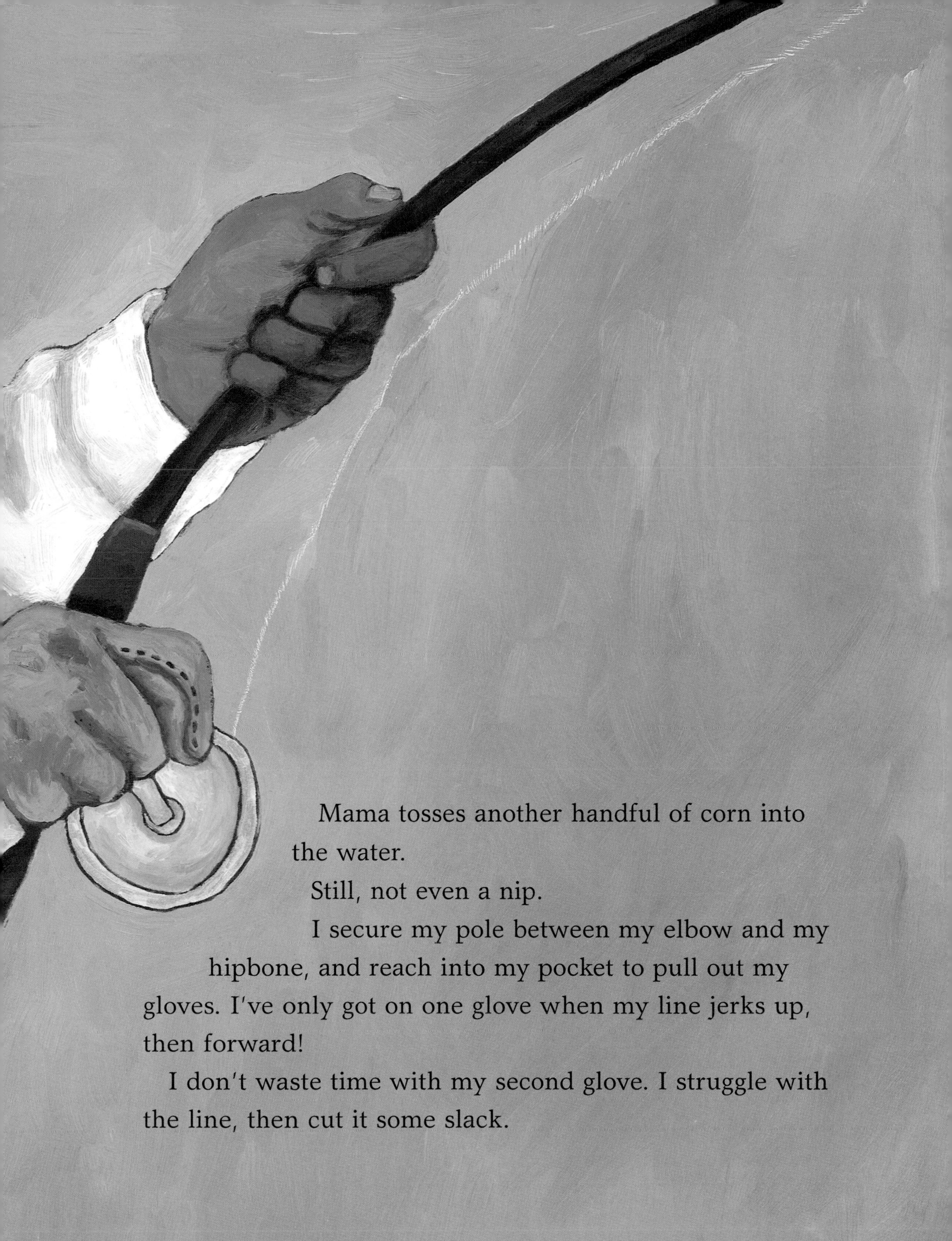

Mama tosses another handful of corn into the water.

Still, not even a nip.

I secure my pole between my elbow and my hipbone, and reach into my pocket to pull out my gloves. I've only got on one glove when my line jerks up, then forward!

I don't waste time with my second glove. I struggle with the line, then cut it some slack.

Finally I reel in the line. Sure enough, I've hooked a nice big carp.

"A keeper," Mama says. "She's beautiful, Reenie! *Beautiful*."

After we've linked our first catch to the carry-chain, Mama's line starts to dance. She's got a feisty one, another keeper. We link her catch with mine, and bait our hooks again. This time I toss the corn kernels, and I can see the carp coming to greet them.

"The news is out that we got corn," Mama says. "The carp are telling all their friends." She laughs.

Pigeon and Mr. Troop haven't caught a thing. When Mr. Troop adjusts the grip on his pole, his reel breaks. He looks like he's trying hard to keep his eyes on fixing his pole, but I see him sneaking glances at Mama and me.

"They always get a catch," I hear Pigeon whine.

"Hush up, boy," Mr. Troop says. "And mind your own business." He stomps off to where he's parked on the other side of a hill. "We just need some pliers from the truck, is all."

Pigeon sets down his pole next to his daddy's and starts sending little stones into the river again. But he's not skipping the stones now—he's flinging them. He blows into his cupped hands to keep them warm. He sniffs hard, like he's trying to hold something in. Then he's back to chucking stones.

But this time he's chucking stones toward Mama and me!

The first one he throws doesn't come close. But the second one nicks me on my knee. I let go of my rod, and rub my leg hard. "*Mama*," I wail.

Mama hugs me to her, helping me ease the sting that's charging up in me. "That boy's hurting," she says gently, her jaw firm. "And he can't help but spread his hurt around."

"Let's just go home, Mama," I snap.

Mama shakes her head no. She gathers up our sack of corn and our rods. We go to a place farther down the river. Mama's quiet.

My line tugs for the second time that day. I've got another carp, a long one, its yellow belly glistening under the morning sun. Pigeon's looking straight at us. Even from where we're fishing, I can see he's working hard not to cry. And there's shame on his face. He looks sorry for what he did.

Mama and I carefully string my fish onto the carry-chain with the others, then I reach into our sack for a new corn kernel to bait my hook.

As soon as I feel my hand curl around those nubby kernels, I know what I've got to do.

I gather up the corn sack and start toward Pigeon, sliding Mama a single backward glance. She nods.

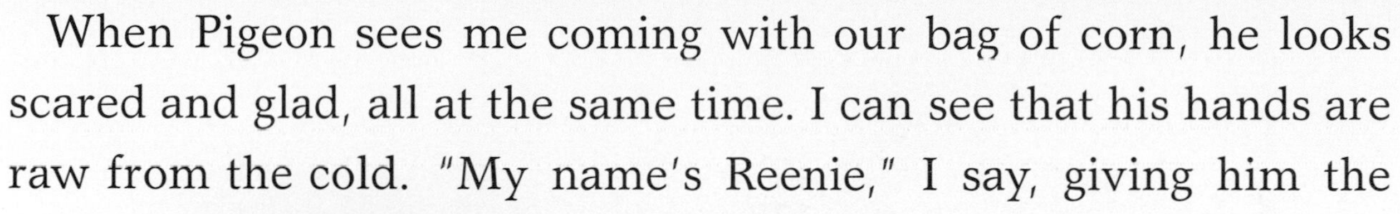

When Pigeon sees me coming with our bag of corn, he looks scared and glad, all at the same time. I can see that his hands are raw from the cold. "My name's Reenie," I say, giving him the glove from my pocket.

"I'm Peter—Peter Troop." He turns his eyes toward the hill. There's no sign of his daddy.

I pull out a fistful of corn from my sack. "Here," I say, offering the kernels to Peter.

"They'll call up the carp," I tell him.

He nods like he already knows. But he won't take the corn.

I bait Peter's hook for him. "Now all you gotta do is wait and *be still*," I say, hoping he'll give his stone throwing a rest.

I leave my small mound of corn on the grass next to Peter, and go back to where Mama's still fishing. When I look sidelong down the river, I can see that Peter's scattering the corn into the water in front of him. Then he sits with his rod just as patient as can be. He's quiet, too. Quiet and still.

When Mr. Troop comes back, Peter's got a snap-tug on his fishing line. Mr. Troop is all giddy. He rushes to help Peter reel in the line.

Mama gives a single nod. "The corn'll do it every time," she says to me.

"Bring her in easy, now," I whisper, struggling to keep my eyes straight ahead on my own bit of water.

When Peter brings in his line, he's got two fish—one on his hook, the other one biting the first fish's tail! Mr. Troop claps Peter's shoulder. "*My* boy," he says. I can see that Peter's proud.

Soon Peter and his daddy pack up their tackle box and head for their truck. I can't see them drive away, but I hear their truck barreling off.

"I guess Lady Luck's smiled on them," Mama says.

"She's smiled double," I say, feeling a little giggle rise up in me.

The next day Mama and I are walking home from church when I spot the Troops' truck crossing the north bend of the hill, near Jim Crow River. When the truck circles around, it's coming toward Mama and me.

Mr. Troop's got his eyes fixed on the road. I look real hard to see Peter, but he's not in the cab next to his daddy.

Then the truck grunts ahead. I turn to watch it pass, and I see Peter sitting in the flatbed. He's looking right at me and waving with the glove I gave him. And I wave back.

Author's Note

Jim Crow was the name of a black character in a popular song composed in the 1830s. The term Jim Crow came into common use in the South in the 1880s, and referred to the separation of blacks and whites in public places. This separation, known as segregation, was the law. Segregation was enforced by signs that indicated "Whites Only" at locations such as restaurants, telephone booths, and rest rooms. Thankfully, Jim Crow laws were abolished by the 1950s.

Though I didn't grow up in the Jim Crow South, where segregation was the law of the land, *Fishing Day* is a story I've lived a thousand times. Throughout my childhood I saw quieter examples of racism's sting. There were no visible "Whites Only" signs in my youth, but segregation still existed, even though its labels weren't posted in public.

I grew up in the Chemung County region of New York State, where fishing was a favorite pastime. I remember summers when my cousins and uncle collected fishing bait and showed me how to force worms or bread chunks onto a hook to catch fish. It was around this time, when I was seven, that I first began to experience prejudice firsthand, mostly at school. My parents, and the relatives who taught me about fishing, gently began to explain the harsh realities of discrimination. Because this time in my life—a time when I experienced my earliest inklings of intolerance—are still so vivid, I chose to set my story of bigotry along a riverbank.

Even then, I was able to understand that nature's places were governed by a higher law, and that a riverbank was free of an imposed divide between people. Still, for me, the separate-sides-of-the-river scenario would play itself out again and again—on the school bus, on the kickball team, in the school cafeteria; where white children stuck together, black children stuck together, and few of us made attempts to mix.

I hated feeling that I was on one side of an invisible fence, and that white children were on the other. Worst of all, I grew to hate my desire to befriend white children whose games and laughter seemed just like mine. And, all the while, I couldn't help but wonder if *they* wanted to be friends with *me*.

I wrote *Fishing Day* in an effort to recast some of the painful times of my childhood. To show that children, if given the chance to formulate their own ideas about differences and tolerance, will often do what is right. *Fishing Day* comes from the belief that generosity and kindness reach beyond all boundaries.

—Andrea Davis Pinkney